Yorks
Legends

Collected by "The Dalesman"

Dalesman Books
1976

The Dalesman Publishing Company Ltd.,
Clapham (via Lancaster), North Yorkshire.

First published 1969
Reprinted 1976

ISBN: 0 85206 348 2

Printed in Great Britain by Galava Printing Company Limited,
Hallam Road, Nelson, Lancashire.

Contents

Illustrations on the front and back covers by E. Jeffrey. End paper drawings by P. B. Rennison. Decorations in the text supplied by Stanley Bond, Tom Bradley, Brian Branster, T. E. Burrill, E. Gower, Elizabeth Gray, Ruth Hedger, Beryl Irving, E. Jeffrey, Fred Lawson, F. S. Sanderson, Ern Shaw, Donald C. Smith, A. Walker, B. Waters, Godfrey Wilson, Alec Wright and readers of *The Dalesman*.

Introduction

YORKSHIRE has an almost inexhaustible hoard of legends and stories with almost every town, village, mountain, dale and moor. Indeed, one wonders if every house more than a few decades old has not a story hidden somewhere among its stones. So a collection like this can only dip into that richness and pick at random among stories that are known and familiar to many and others that have been forgotten and are worth re-telling.

These stories can be read in several ways. They can be entertaining footnotes to north-country history and topography, to its folk-lore and customs. The legends of a land can illuminate its true history with a light of their own which throws into strong relief aspects of bygone life and which might have been unknown or overlooked. Even though they are far-fetched and some distance from the truth, such legends can often represent the beliefs and ideals of the community from which they spring. A county which forgets its legendary tales is poor indeed, and this little collection may remind us of Yorkshire's rich and varied store.

—**The Dalesman**

1 The Dales

Out of the Depths

WHEN men had little inclination to wander into our gloomy limestone caves, or descend the eerie shafts on the fells, a host of tales were told of trolls and boggarts, fairies and elves. Narrow limestone gorges were the lairs of ferocious beasts, including the barguest—a spectral hound—which lived in Trollers Gill, near Appletreewick. To be about the limestone country after dark was to court trouble and, perhaps, disaster.

We laugh at the quaint notions of the past, yet if you wander in limestone country when the sun is dipping behind the western horizon and the shadows are long and gloomy, you will not pass without a shiver of excitement the shafts in which water laps or gurgles, or the cave mouths lying dark and silent, or the gills and valleys in which a stone disturbed by a sheep can give you an impression that a monster is tearing down the slopes.

Today, says the scientist, there is a rational explanation for everything—but is there? What does the scientist make of the experience of three different men on the heights of Greenhow where, some say, the ghosts of "t'Owd Man"—collective name for generations of lead miners—still wanders?

A member of a cave survey group was camping at Stump Cross one night when there was a full moon aloft. He heard the sound of clogs coming down the road about midnight and left his car to investigate. The sound came nearer, passed him and went towards Greenhow. There was no-one about. Mr. George Gill, guide to Stump Cross Caverns, says that in 1939, when he was living at Greenhow, he heard the sound of clogs outside the house and noticed that the moon was full. The clogs sounded on the gravel of the road, then on the cobble stones by its side, and finally on the gritstone slab at the door. There was no-one to be seen, either by himself or his wife. Another local man heard ghostly clog sounds. This time the sounds indicated that a man was stepping from a bicycle prior to walking beside it. When the man looked in the direction of the sounds there was no-one about.

Ancient legends of boggarts and spirits residing in the caverns of north-west Yorkshire have left their legacy in the cave names of today, as in the various Boggart Holes, Rumbling Hole or Fairies' Workshop, and the older form of Helln, now Alum Pot or "mouth of Hell!" The legends faded and man became more curious and more adventurous. Hurtle Pot, just behind the little church in Chapel-le-Dale, was said to be the haunt of a boggart which drowned its prey in a pool at the bottom. Trollers Gill has a name which associates it with the wicked little dwarfs of the cave, the trolls, which feature in the folk-lore of Scandinavia. What stories lie behind underground systems named Fairy Hole, Batty Wife Hole, Dog Hole, Antler Hole, Death's Head Hole, Lost Johns' (who were the two Johns involved?), Witches Cave or Robin Hood's Cave?

The Hand of Glory

EVERY good Yorkshireman has heard of the Hand of Glory, although not all could tell the story of this strange affair even though it has been handed down in many versions. Here is one which is as good as the next although its details may be contradicted by the next man who tells it.

One cold and wild October night (it must always begin thus) in the year 1797 (here there may be a difference of date), the innkeeper of the *Spital Inn* on Stainmore, a dreary northern upland, sat by the fireside discussing his takings from travellers to Brough Hill Fair which had been that day. Apart from Fair days the inn was usually deserted in the winter months, and the innkeeper, George Alderson, his wife and son, and their maid-of-all-work, Bella, were the only folk known to be in the district for many miles around. So there was no little surprise in the family circle when, on this of all nights, above the roar of the gale and the crackle of logs on the hearth, a knock was heard at the door. It was Bella who answered it cautiously for none knew who might be outside. But her caution gave way to even greater surprise when she found the old and bent figure of a woman on the doorstep.

Hidden in a great cloak and hood little could be seen of this strange visitor even when she came into the inn. And as she refused to doff her garments, only her weather-beaten hands and furrowed features could be studied. She refused both food and bed that were offered to her and declared that she would rest for the night in an armchair by the fireside. Finding no response to their attempts at conversation, the innkeeper and his wife and son soon retired, leaving Bella to keep the old woman company. It was while bolting and barring the door for the night that the girl noticed under the hem of the stranger's skirt the gaiters of a horseman, and her fears were heightened when she recognised in the surly "good-night" the tones of a man's voice.

Bella stretched herself out on a low settee in the room and feigned sleep. For a while there was silence, then suddenly the figure in the chair moved, rose to its feet and listened intently. It was no longer the bent figure of an old woman but the tall, powerful frame of a man. From the folds of the cloak the stranger took a brown, withered hand and the stump of a candle, which "she" lit at the fire and placed in the hand. Then to the trembling

Bella's horror the figure approached and, stooping over her, passed this ghastly human candlestick before the girl's tight-closed eyes murmuring in a strange masculine voice, the incantation:

Let those who rest more deeply sleep;
Let those who wake their vigils keep.

Then the light moved away, and peeping through her eye-lashes Bella saw the figure place the hand on the table and heard the same voice continue:

Oh Hand of Glory shed thy light;
Direct us to our spoil tonight.

There was a pause while the "woman" moved to the window and parted the curtains. Then once more the voice continued:

Flash out thy blaze, O skeleton hand,
And guide the feet of our trusty band.

The voice had hardly ceased when the candle blazed up in a vivid flame. The "woman" walked to the door, unbarred it and, standing on the step, blew a long blast on a whistle. The trembling maid summoned up all her courage. In an instant she crossed the room, gave the figure on the step a push into the road below and slammed and barred the door. Rushing to the innkeeper's bedroom she shouted and shook him, but in vain for he slumbered on. Nor did she get any response from his wife and son.

Meanwhile there was a great hubbub at the door. Threats and oaths could be heard above the gale and voices called to her to open the door or see it rammed in. In desperation the girl thought of the candle still burning in the Hand of Glory on the table. Catching up a cup of milk she dashed it on the light and plunged the house into darkness. Almost in a moment George Alderson and his son hurried in to learn the cause of the disturbance—their trance was broken. A crash on the door and voices and threats outside warned of their danger. A blunderbus was brought and pointed through the window at the mob outside, and at the first shot there were cries of pain. A second shot brought a parley. The same strange voice called out that if the Hand of Glory was returned the band would disperse without further harm. But by this time the Aldersons had procured more firearms and they replied with a volley that sent the mob, wounded and un-wounded flying in panic from the inn.

For the rest of that night the innkeeper and his son sat with firearms in their hands waiting for a return of the marauders but no sign of them appeared. Nor did anyone ever know the identity of the strange nocturnal visitor nor of "her" companions. For many years the Aldersons kept the gruesome withered hand as a memento of this strange happening. And for long the story was told on winter nights in homes and inns in the wild country around Stainmore.

The Grisedale Pie

THEY have a pungent way in Wensleydale of summing up a person in a very few words. If, for example, you have a too frequent visitor you say of him, "He's like a Grisedale pie, sure to come again." The phrase is explained by a legend about Grisedale, a small valley at the head of the dale. John Routh, who wrote a *Guide to Wensleydale* many years ago, relates the legend thus: "A potato pie was once made in Grisedale and, being forgotten, was not brought out for half a year, when the potatoes are said to have taken root and grown out of the top of the crust. The pie was frequently afterwards placed upon the table, but nobody seemed fond of it, hence the origin of the saying."

A Queen Walks

NAPPA Hall, near Askrigg in Wensleydale, although now a farm, was the old manor house of the great Metcalfe family. It is also not very far from Bolton Castle, where Mary, Queen of Scots, was a prisoner, although she was allowed to ride under escort round the countryside and even on occasion to spend a night or two away as a guest of local halls. Two nights were spent in this way at Nappa, as the guest of Sir Christopher Metcalfe, and it is said that her spirit still visits the hall. In *About Yorkshire*, written by Thomas and Katherine Macquoid and published in 1883, a letter is quoted from a lady who stayed at the hall in 1878:

"I was in the hall playing hide-and-seek with the farmer's little girl, a child about four years old. The hall was dimly lighted by a fire and by the light from a candle in a room in the east tower. While at play someone entered the hall from the lower end, and walked towards the dais. Thinking it was the farmer's wife I ran after her, and was going to touch her when she turned round, and I saw her face: it was very lovely. Her dress seemed to be made of black velvet. After looking at me for a moment, she went on and disappeared through the door leading to the winding stone staircase in the angle turret of the west tower. Her face, figure, and general appearance reminded me of portraits of Mary, Queen of Scots."

At the time of this vision the bedstead slept in by the Queen was still at Nappa Hall.

The Giant of Penhill

THE legend of the Giant of Penhill is a story comparable to the great Scandinavian sagas. Once it was told on winter evenings round Yorkshire hearths and was handed down from generation to generation. Today it is almost forgotten.

In the castle of Penhill, in the heart of Wensleydale, there lived a giant, a descendant of the mighty Thor. He was known and feared in all the country round, for he was a brutal and cruel land-owner and delighted in ill-treating the people. His only other pleasures were in his herd of swine and his dog, Wolfhead. Day after day he would stand and count the herd as his swineherds and his dog marshalled the beasts to pass before him, and woe unto his followers if one beast was missing or was lame or was not in good condition.

While travelling from one part of his land to another one day to inspect his herds he saw a poor but lovely shepherdess, watching her small flock on the hillside. Here was a chance for amusement that he could not let pass, and he called up his dog and set it on to worry the sheep. The poor maiden pleaded that the little flock represented the entire wealth of her father and mother and that their loss would mean ruin. But the giant only laughed more heartily until the terrified girl fled into the forest.

Here, in the giant's view was still livelier sport, and he sent Wolfhead in pursuit of the girl, he following more slowly as his great bulk demanded. When he arrived at a clearing in the wood he found the girl lying helpless, with her clothes torn off and with bleeding limbs, while the great dog growled and played with her as a cat plays with a mouse. As the giant watched and laughed, the girl rallied all her strength for a last effort and picking up a stone crashed it down on the dog's head. The dog howled with pain and the giant, in a rage, raised his club and slew the girl. He then bent down and annointed the bruised dog with the warm blood of the dying girl.

When the news of his crime spread among the people, there was great discontent and many threats and murmurings. One day a boar was missing from the giant's herd and in a mighty passion of anger the giant blamed all those round him for their negligence. He sent his terrified swineherds flying for their lives and with a brutal kick at his dog ordered it to find the missing boar, cursing the creature meanwhile for its carelessness in guarding his herds. Wolfhead slunk away, nor could the giant that night or any other persuade the dog to return. It would sit out of range of arrow or stone and howl at the castle, and though the giant raged and fumed it would no longer obey his call to come to heel.

Meanwhile the missing boar had been found in the forest with an arrow through its heart, and the giant's anger with the people knew no bounds. He summoned every man and boy who could use a bow to assemble at the castle gate and threatened terrible tortures for those who failed to appear. In a dead silence when the company had gathered he called for the man who had made and shot the arrow which had killed his beast. But not a voice replied. In a wrath he demanded that anyone who knew the culprit or recognised the arrow should declare all they knew. Again there was silence.

"By the Great God Thor, my ancestor," the giant declared, "I will find out. Before sunset tomorrow every father of a male child must bring here the last born male in his family. Then will their death cries open your lips and make you confess. Away with you all."

But before the great company could move, an old man with a long grey beard stepped forward, leaning on a curious carved stick. "Hold, O mighty giant," he said, "and tell us what you propose to do with our children tomorrow."

"I will give you your answer from my bow," retorted the giant, "if you dare to question me. I will do what I please."

The Seer of Carperby—for such was the old man—raised his stick in warning. "If you so much as spill one drop of blood or make a single child cry out with fear, then thou shalt never enter thy castle again dead or alive. I speak that which I know," he said.

But the giant laughed, turned on his heel and strode into his castle while the people dispersed. On the following day a sorrowing company, with children of all ages, gathered again at the castle of Penhill. And there they found the ancient Seer, who bade them be joyful for no harm would befall them. Inside the castle the giant sharpened his battle-axe and watched the people gathering round the walls. He was about to leave the castle when an old retainer begged audience of him and besought him not to venture forth. "I dreamed last night," he said, "that nine black ravens flew nine times round the castle and lighted upon it and there cawed nine times. And a raven in the likeness of the old Seer was the leader of them. This means great evil, O giant."

For answer the giant felled the retainer with his battle-axe and strode out of the room. Bleeding and dazed, the old servant gathered straw and peat and chairs and tables and piled them in a great heap and then, seizing a faggot from the hearth, set fire to the pile. Meanwhile, the giant strode down to the castle gate and at every stride he found nine of his beloved swine dead in a row. Row upon row they laid, stirring him to a passion so that he could scarce contain himself. Arriving at the gate he snatched at a babe lying in its mother's arms with such fury that the child shrieked with fear. He would have killed it outright had not the old Seer stepped forward and seized the child, pointing with his stick to the castle. "Look," he cried, "my words have come true."

As the giant turned he saw a vast cloud of smoke arise from Penhill and out of the smoke nine great flames leaped up into the sky. Swinging his battle-axe the giant turned to slay the old Seer, but as he turned another sight met his eyes, his axe fell from his hands, and he became speechless. A wraith-like

form approached and he saw it was in the shape of the lovely shepherdess whom he had killed. In her hand was a leash at the end of which Wolfhead strained to get at the giant. Step by step the giant retreated until the wraith slipped the leash and the dog flew at the throat of the giant. He stepped back and with the dog upon him went hurtling over the great precipice, and nevermore was Wensleydale troubled by a descendant of Thor.

The Woman in Black

COVERDALE, as befits one of the most secluded of the Yorkshire Dales, has a reputation for ghosts and unexplained incidents. It also has legends probably founded on fact. The story of the woman in black is just one example.

There was a long period when Coverdale folk were terrified at the thought of walking by night from the church to a place on Middleham Moor known as "Courting Wall Corner," because somewhere there they might meet a woman draped in mourning and shaking her head in anguish. On one

Coverham, Coverdale

occasion some passengers in a trap saw the figure and, not knowing of her reputation, asked her to open a gate across the road. But the figure vanished. Apparently the facts were that the woman had had two lovers, and eventually agreed to elope with one of them. The other lover discovered the scheme and murdered the woman, burying the body on the moor. So she returned to haunt the dale. Years later peat-gatherers on the moor found the skeleton of a woman not far below the surface. A piece of black cloth was unearthed close by. So did the legend have a basis of truth?

New Ground

THERE was an old Dales belief (shared by gypsies) that the Devil always claimed as his due the first body buried in new ground. Hence the story told of a burial ground at the top end of Nidderdale where the churchyard became full and a piece of adjoining land had to be taken in. It was carefully walled round and the bishop consecrated it. But the vicar was dismayed to find that none of his parishioners were willing to bury their dead in the new ground. Those dying pleaded not to be the first to be interred there, for fear of the Devil. This difficult situation might have continued but for the finding, one winter's day of a tramp frozen to death on the moors. The parishioners brought him to the vicar and said, "Bury him in t'new ground." And following some formalities this was done, and the parishioners died happily ever after.

Brimham Rocks

TRAVELLERS in Nidderdale have long marvelled at the gritty monstrosities of Brimham Rocks breaking into the skyline. All manner of stories have been told about them linking them with Druids, with Mother Shipton, and with the Devil himself.

The most romantic of these legends concerns a lovesick young man, Edwin, and his girl-friend Julia, who had suffered from parent trouble and decided to elope. They slipped away from their homes and fled across the moors, pursued by an angry father. Melodramatically, he caught up with them as they stood marooned on the top of an isolated crag. All was apparently lost. The young couple decided to make a final leap together into space and die hand in hand.

They jumped, and by great good fortune (or the aid of a

Brimham Rocks

fairy in old versions) landed safely on the ground. The girl's father was so impressed with this miraculous escape that he embraced them both, consented to their marriage and they lived happily ever afterwards. The guide today will, if you ask him, point out the Lovers' Rock from which they jumped. He will also point out the Wishing Stone which contains a hole into which you place the middle finger of your right hand and wish, and the Rocking Stone, which will only move if pushed by an honest man. It is said that no Yorkshireman has yet achieved this.

Wharfedale Morals

VICE and virtue are displayed with proper moral endings in two Wharfedale villages not far apart. At Threshfield long ago there lived a miller who, like all millers from the time of Chaucer, had a bad reputation for pilfering from the mouths of his customers' sacks—a custom known as "mouthering" which was best carried out by a miller with smooth hands. Hence the old Yorkshire saying: "Honest millers have hairy palms." However, the dishonest miller of Threshfield made much out of his evil ways and would have so continued but returning from market late one night mistook a wandering

goat for the dreaded barguest (or phantom dog). He was so overwhelmed by fear that he vowed he would be honest afterwards. So vice became virtue.

Appletreewick, which is known locally as "Aptrick," was the birthplace of Yorkshire's Dick Whittington, whose virtue brought him great reward. Willie Craven was a poor lad in the village until he decided to go to London to make a fortune. He travelled there (without cat) in a curious cart, became a draper's assistant, made a large fortune as a mercer and achieved the dignities recorded on a stone at Burnsall church which he had repaired: "Sir William Craven, knight and alderman of the citie of London. And late Lord Mayre of the same. Anno dm. 1612." His son married a Queen of Bohemia. Could virtue do more?

The Five-fold Echo

THERE is a legend of an echo which nowadays no one can find, although thousands of people visit the site every year. It began when a clergyman on holiday visited Malham Cove in Airedale in or about 1830. He took a guide with him, as was then the custom, and he described what happened: "While praying vows to the genius of this sequestered place, my guide at my direction, struck up a tune on a clarinet. Music at such a time, I think, is in its place, and is most calculated either to soothe the broken spirit or enkindle the nobler passions of the mind . . ."

More to the point, however, the musical clergyman distinctly heard the music echo five times when played "from a certain stone near the great cliff. It has a most pleasing effect in a fine summer's evening." Today the five-fold echo is unknown, even to local folk.

Watery Grave

IN the churchyard at Kirkby Malham there is a grave with a tiny archway in the headstone through which a stream runs. At one time, it is said, there was an inscription on the stone, "As water parted us in life, so it shall in death." They will tell you in the village that the grave is of a sea captain and his wife whose married life was made unhappy because he was away so long at sea. When he died, his wife declared that as water had parted them so long in life so it should in death, and the grave was so designed that she should be buried on the other side of the stream from her husband. Unfortunately at her death it was found impossible to excavate her grave as desired because of the underlying rock, so she was buried above her husband. But her intentions were made clear by the inscription.

Witch of Clapdale

THOSE who make the ascent of Ingleborough from Clapham, in Craven, can follow a track which passes Clapdale Hall, once known as Clapdale Castle and described by an old historian as "very strong." In the castle there once lived John de Clapham and not far away, at the foot of Trow Gill (which

Clapham

you can climb on the way up Ingleborough), there was a tiny cottage in which lived Dame Alice Ketyll, his foster-mother. She was troubled by the poor fortune of her foster-son and after much anguish decided to call upon the Devil for aid. Following Satanic precedent, the Devil called upon one Robyn Artisson to be her familiar spirit who would assist. She had to promise to sweep the old Clapham bridge, which stands near the church, between Compline and Curfew—the dust towards the castle—and repeat the lines:

Into the house of John, my sonne,
Hie all the wealth of Clapham towne.

At midnight she was to take nine red cocks, freshly killed, and place them in a ring round her on the bridge, and to call her familiar spirit there by name. There would be a flash of light and her familiar spirit would appear—only to be seen by herself—and he would do anything she wanted for her foster-son. If the nine red cocks were not offered on any night, only once more would the Devil assist her, then she would be his.

"Dost thou accept these conditions?" asked the Devil, as he produced the bond. After much hesitation (not unnatural as the bond was written in letters of fire) she accepted and signed the bond with her blood. The Devil whistled and the familiar spirit appeared, with a grin on his face for he knew that to find nine red cocks each night would be impossible. So Dame Alice became a witch and used her power, while it lasted, to aid the Lord of Clapdale Castle, though in return her soul went to the Devil.

Theologian's Wit

DOCTOR William Paley, the famous theologian, was educated at Giggleswick School, where his father was headmaster. The school still has a Paley House. Paley was an enthusiastic horseman but a poor rider and frequently suffered falls. Whenever his father heard a bump on the ground he merely glanced around and called out: "Take care of thi' money, lad." Many stories have become legendary about the theologian's wit as he rose to fame. He was debating with a solemn group of Cambridge students what was the highest good (*summum bonum*) of human life. After much discussion he declared: "I differ from you all, gentlemen. The highest good in human life consists in reading *Tristram Shandy*, in blowing with a pair of bellows into your shoes in hot weather, and in roasting potatoes in the ashes under the grate in cold."

On another occasion when he was at a dinner to celebrate his first church appointment as vicar he called out gaily, "Waiter, shut down the window at the back of my chair and open another behind some curate's."

Pudsay's Leap

IN the valley of the river Ribble, so close to Lancashire that its post-town is Clitheroe, is a bit of Yorkshire that is often forgotten. There are deep woods, high limestone cliffs, and lonely stretches of the Ribble where rare wild birds and flowers can be found. There is a particular cliff marked as Rainsber Scar on the map, but known locally as Pudsay's Leap. Bolton Hall nearby was the home of the Pudsay family for many generations, and enough stories are told of them to fill this book. Here is the one which gave its name to the Leap.

It concerns a Pudsay of the time of the first Queen Elizabeth who was said to be his godmother. He was a man fond of good company and much entertaining, but like many others before and since found it a very expensive hobby—so much so that his funds ran out and the debts came in. Being a wise man, Pudsay bethought himself of two elves, Lob and Michael, who lived in those deep woods near the hall and had a reputation for even greater wisdom. He consulted them and they told him to go to a particular corner of his own estate where he would find a useful vein of silver, and it was not long before he was busy mining the ore, treating it at the water mill, and turning out silver shillings galore.

But you cannot keep a thing like that quiet. The authorities at York heard of this illegal minting of coins and sent a posse of soldiers to arrest him. Once more Pudsay was in difficulties and consulted those knowing elves who promptly gave him a silver bit for his horse. This, they said, would ensure him a safe passage and his horse would never tire. When the posse of waiting soldiers reached the hall he jumped on to the waiting horse and dashed off through the woods, followed by the troopers. They chased him to the river's brink where the water flowed 90 feet below the cliff and thought they had captured him. But with a cry of "Better a leap from my own grey rock than from the gallows at York," Pudsay and his horse bounded over the cliff. The elves' bit proved its value. Neither horse nor rider were hurt and Pudsay was able to ride on to London where the Queen agreed to pardon him provided he did not go into the coin-minting business again. So Pudsay's Leap became a legend for all time.

Shepherd Lord

IN the peaceful courtyard of the old castle of Skipton, when the stones reflect the colour of the sky and the venerable yew tree in the centre gives a warmth and a sense of life to this historic place, legend and reality merge. Was the story of the "Shepherd Lord" fact or fiction?

It was in one of those long, low rooms overlooking the courtyard that the proud and handsome Lady Clifford sat with her three children, and attendants busy with distaff and spinning wheel, on a spring evening in the year 1461. Not many days before, on Palm Sunday, the fearful battle of Towton between the Houses of York and Lancaster had been fought, but as yet no news had reached the castle. Lord Clifford, as a supporter of the King, Henry VI, and Queen Margaret, had placed his forces at the disposal of the Red Rose against the rebel Yorkists, and they had been to the forefront at Towton. There were many anxious hearts that night among the homesteads of Craven, and not the least of these was Lady Clifford's. As the little company sat and spun and waited, a trumpet sounded and a few moments later a knight, who gave the name of Sir John de Barnoldswick, was admitted and made obeisance. "Whence comest thou and with what tidings, Sir Knight?" asked Lady Clifford anxiously.

"I come from the field of battle, lady, and my tidings are evil," was the reply. Only after much questioning and with great hesitation did the worthy knight disclose that the Lancastrian cause had lost at Towton field, that the King and Queen had fled, and that Lord Clifford was dead from an arrow wound in the throat. Despite the hesitation of the knight, the shock was very great for Lady Clifford. She cared less for herself than for her children and home, for in those days the death of a great Lord was often followed by the extermination of his family and the sequestration of their estates. And Lord Clifford was not loved by the Yorkists. Her fears were not unnecessary; as soon as the new King Edward of York was on the throne orders went forth for the handing over of Skipton Castle and the estates of Lord Clifford to a supporter of the new King, and rumours came that the children were to be placed in captivity.

Disguised as a farmer's wife, Lady Clifford set out with one or two attendants and the children to her father's estate at Londesborough near Market Weighton, passing through Otley, Tadcaster and York, but keeping as much as possible to the by-roads. They arrived safely and there remained some time until news came that the Yorkists, having discovered that Skipton Castle was empty, had determined to find the young Cliffords and that Londesborough was suspected. Once more Lady Clifford was compelled to make plans for her children's safety. Her youngest child, Elizabeth, she placed in the care of a household, so that she could be passed off as a child of one of the retainers. The next, Richard, was sent across the sea to Flanders and the eldest, Henry, was sent off with a loyal and trusted shepherd and his wife to a remote part of Cumberland, where the roads were few and travellers rare.

It was there among the fells that the boy grew up as a shepherd lad, living simply, observing the seasons and the stars, and acquiring much rural wisdom. Meanwhile, almost unknown to him, political fortunes turned again. Henry was called from the pastures of Cumberland to take possession of the family home, and once more the banner of the Cliffords floated in the breeze over Skipton Castle. Legend tells us he was not happy in the transformation. The crude splendour of the castle and court was not to his liking. So the "Shepherd Lord" as he was called, retired whenever possible to the Forest of Barden, where he built the lodge now known as Barden Tower. There he discussed astronomy and the theories he had formed in his lonely watches on the Cumberland fells, with the monks of Bolton close by. Even here, however, the calls of politics and affairs of State reached him, and like his predecessors he went forth to do battle. In the year 1513 at the age of 60 he held a command at Flodden Field and acquitted himself well:

From Penigent to Pendle Hill,
From Linton to Long Addingham,
And all that Craven coats did till
They with the lusty Clifford came.

Lady Clifford died at Londesborough in the year 1491 and was there buried near the altar of the church. The "Shepherd Lord" survived Flodden and lived until his seventieth year and his remains lie with those of his ancestors in the peaceful church at Bolton, not far from his quiet retreat at Barden.

The Craven Heifer

THE Craven Heifer takes its place in history with the Durham Ox and other monstrosities of size but it had its own unusual legends. First its size, which may be legendary. The heifer had a girth in the middle of 10 ft. 2 in. and at the loin of 9 ft. 11 in., with a height at the shoulder of 5 ft. 2 in., and a length from nose to rump of 11 ft. 2 in. Born in 1807, its owner was the Rev. William Carr, incumbent of Bolton Abbey church, but it passed into other hands and was put on show at fairs and shows in the principal towns of Yorkshire and Lancashire, with legends about its eating capacity and weight growing all the time.

Eventually, when doubtless the meat would be a little tough from much travel, the Heifer was made the prize at a "main" of cocks, was won by a Huddersfield man and the carcase disposed of for a shilling a pound. That was not the end of its fame however. So much of a sensation had it caused when on show that several hostelries changed their name to "Craven Heifer," and eventually it appeared on the notes of the Craven Bank which had previously carried an engraving of Castleberg Rock, Settle.

2 The Urban West Riding

Thirsty Lions

IF you travel the Keighley to Skipton road and glance up the hillside when you reach the Airedale village of Kildwick—which has a bridge over the river that was built by the canons of Bolton Abbey in 1300– you may notice a fine old hall, not as old as the bridge, but dating back to the 17th century. If your eyesight is good you may notice stone lions guarding the gateway. Still more exciting, come back and watch them again when Kildwick church clock strikes midnight and you will see them descend from their perch and walk down to the river for a drink. So the locals will tell you!

London by the Aire

CANADA, Philadelphia and New York are all local place-names that could be found in the hillside village of Rawdon in Airedale, and probably originated from the travels of local mill-owners. But Little London, a part of the village, is more puzzling, as there is in it a London Lane and a Lombard Street. Over the years a story has grown that a Rawdon man once travelled to London to find fame and fortune. His fame is lost in the mists of time, but he brought his fortune back to his native village and invested it in a suburb which he called Little London. It sounds as good a story as any.

The Tongueless Head

BRADFORD'S coat of arms, granted in 1847, is surmounted by a tongueless boar's head crest, and thereby hangs a tale. Long ago when Bradford was a small community with a church, a manor house and a few cottages surrounded by dense forest a great, fierce, wild boar appeared and caused havoc among the community. No-one dared go into the woods for food or fuel and it was dangerous even for the people to leave their houses. So serious became the menace that the lord of the manor promised his lovely daughter in marriage to whoever would slay the animal.

A page in the lord's service who was enamoured of the girl determined to win the reward. He first spent many days quietly digging a pit in front of the den of the sleeping monster. Then he provided himself with a spear and a sword. When all was ready he made a great noise in front of the animal's den and himself paraded up and down. The boar woke up angrily, rushed furiously out, and fell into the pit, whereupon the page speared it to death and then used the sword to remove its tongue as evidence of his success. Then he set off to claim his reward.

Alack, another page also had a passion for the Lord's daughter. He set out to kill the boar and, finding it dead in the pit, cut off its head and hurried off to claim the lady. He arrived early and was about to receive his reward when the first page arrived with the tongue, pointing out that a head without a tongue proved nothing, but that a tongue without a head proved he was the killer. So he became the Lord's son-in-law, and Bradford depicted the tongueless head in its crest.

Treasure at Kirkstall

THERE is no lack of buried treasure for the finding in Yorkshire– under Richmond Castle, under Middleham Castle, indeed under almost every castle in the county. If the sceptics laugh, well, didn't they laugh at Mother Shipton's predictions? If you are not a sceptic then you may like to know of a fortune awaiting someone at Kirkstall Abbey, near Leeds. The facts are as plain as tradition can make them.

It is not so long ago that an old chap was working in the meadows of the ruined abbey when he saw by the way the shadow of the old tower fell across the grass that it was time he knocked off for his mid-day snack. He ate his meat and drank his bottle of home-brewed beer and then thought he would stretch his back. He wandered round the abbey and came across a hole under the ruins he had not noticed before. Full of a Yorkshireman's curiosity he clambered down and found an entry into a passage which, in his own words, "led to a great houseplace." It was dark and eerie down there but he went on to discover "a gurt fire blazing on t'hearthstone," and in one corner of the room "a gurt black horse." It promptly whinnied at him.

Then, behind the horse, was a vast oak chest and "on t'top of' t'kist a gurt black cock." It promptly crowed at him. But he was not easily put off by the animal noises, particularly as he had the notion that any big oak chest must contain treasure, as every story book tells. So, as bold as "t'brass" he expected to find he strode up to the chest and began to lift the lid. The horse whinnied higher, the black cock crowed louder, and an old owl he hadn't seen shrieked like a gabble-ratchet at him and something "catched him a fair clip ower t'head" and laid him flat. When he came to he was lying on the ground beside the abbey, and although he searched and searched and better searched he "nivver fun yon hoile ageean." So the treasure is still waiting for a bolder man.

Royal Captive

THE street name, King Charles' Croft, in the centre of Leeds was for a long time a reminder that nearby stood Red House where that king was once held as a prisoner—and refused a chance to escape. Ralph Thoresby, the historian of Leeds, tells the story, though how much is history and how

Old Leeds

much is legend is uncertain. Here is his account:

"When Charles I was being conveyed a prisoner to London by his gaoler, Cornet Joyce, he was lodged in the Red House here. A maidservant of the house entreated him to put on her clothes and make his escape, assuring him that she would conduct him in the dark out of the garden door into a back alley called Land's Lane, and thence to a friend's house from which he might make his escape to France. The King however, declined the woman's offer with many thanks, and gave her a token so that on the site of that token his son would reward her. After the Restoration the woman presented the token to the King, and told him the story. The King enquired whence she came; she said, 'From Leeds in Yorkshire'; whether she had a husband; she replied, 'Yes'; what was his calling?; she said, 'An under-bailiff.' 'Then,' said the King, 'he shall be chief bailiff in Yorkshire.'"

The Great Boffin Hoax

HOW many of the older generation of Leeds people remember the great Boffin hoax which began in Leeds? Old Liberals ought certainly to recall it, for it was a great mystery in the party. It may still be a mystery to some.

It arose from an article which the late Augustine Birrell wrote in a weekly paper in which, wishing to illustrate an argument, he used the name of a purely fictitious character, Tobias Boffin. Immediately there came a letter from a very angry correspondent of that name, purporting to be a Unitarian minister but actually non-existent except in the minds of certain humorist friends of Mr. Birrell's who created him to puzzle the writer.

It happened that a meeting of the National Liberal Federation was about to be held in Leeds, so Sir Robert Hudson, who was in the conspiracy and was an important Liberal official, had the name of the "Rev. Tobias Boffin" inserted in the conference papers next to that of Herbert Samuel as being among those attending. The name actually appeared in a number of newspaper accounts. To carry the joke still further, a letter appeared in the *Liberal Magazine* from the same fictitious worthy objecting to the use of his name by Mr. Birrell, and the plotters even went so far as to announce in *The Times* a marriage by "the Rev. Tobias Boffin, B.A., father of the bride."

Mr. Birrell and other Liberals were greatly perturbed by the matter, and it is said that, although Mr. Birrell at times suspected a hoax, he also consulted several University lists to find the name of Boffin among the B.A.s. His confusion was increased when, on one occasion, a card was sent up to him in the House by "Mr. Boffin," asking for an interview. When he went to the Lobby he was told that the reverend gentleman "had just left."

Later a "Boffin Book" was published telling the whole story of the hoax and illustrated with sketches of Boffin at the ages of seven, 37, and "present day." But there may still be some who believe the Rev. Tobias Boffin, B.A., to be a real person.

What's in a Name?

THERE is a curious link between the Clapham family of North Craven and Potternewton Park in Leeds, if a recent legend is to be believed. The story goes that one day a century or so ago a Mr. Thomas Clapham, who resided at the mansion of Potternewton, was called on by a solicitor who had journeyed from Settle to Leeds to inform him he had been left an estate worth between £4,000 and £5,000 a year (very considerable for those days). The benefactor was Thomas Clapham, of whom the Leeds man had never heard and whom he had never seen.

Suspecting a bad joke, the legatee made inquiries and found that the will and bequest were both in order if eccentric. Apparently the benefactor had, a long time before, seen a carriage and pair at some public function. He enquired whose it was and was told that by coincidence it belonged to a Mr. Thomas Clapham. This tickled his sense of humour and he promptly decided to make out his will in favour of the unknown namesake. "Won't the old devil stare when he gets it?" he muttered with glee as he signed the document.

Fire!

MANY good stories are told in Yorkshire about its fire brigades in the days when these were purely local institutions. They are legendary of course, like many stories about well-loved things, and they are mainly concerned with the discomfiture of the brigade. For example, the story of the great inspection and march-past of the Brighouse Fire Brigade which took place a generation or two ago. The whole force turned out and was inspected by its chief, resplendent in a pair of white gloves. He then roared out the order to form fours. There was a shuffling in the ranks, and one of the brigade ventured a protest. "Nay George," he said, "tha' knows there's nobbut three of us without thee."

"All right, then," said the Superintendent of the Brighouse Fire Brigade sadly, "fall in, two deep."

There is the equally legendary story of how the old Thorne horse-drawn fire brigade (now equipped with a smart motor engine) was once called out, and after waiting an hour for the horse to turn up, they decided to push the engine to the fire themselves. When they got there they found that the Doncaster Fire Brigade had put the fire out and had gone home.

The Soldier of Trybergh

A TOUCHING story comes from Trybergh, near Sheffield, where you can still see the remains in the village of two ancient

crosses. One of these, St. Leonard's Cross, commemorates Leonard de Reresby who fought in one of the Crusades and was taken prisoner by the Saracens, and was held captive for seven years. By ancient custom his wife was allowed to marry again after this time and planned a new wedding. Either by the mercy of the Saracens, according to one version, or by the strength of his own prayers, according to another, Leonard was set free. He was found, according to both versions, lying fettered in a nearby field just as the church bells were ringing for his wife's second marriage. Many years later he was canonised.

Pontefract Cakes

LIQUORICE root, so long associated with Pontefract, has a remarkable history, part fact and part legend. Ancient peoples must have known the root as a medicine for it is mentioned on the clay tablets of Babylon and recorded by the early Egyptians, Greeks and Romans. It was imported into this country for the same purpose in the 16th century, but many folk have wondered how it became a confection.

The story goes that a certain worthy schoolmaster of Pontefract was on holiday at the coast at the time of the Spanish Armada. Wandering along the beach one day he picked up a bundle of twigs washed ashore from a wrecked galleon, and it occurred to him that they would serve the purpose and save the expense of birch-twigs as a means of inflicting punishment. He soon had occasion to try them out on his return to Pontefract and so effective was his new "cane" that his boys were driven to pick up shreds from his twigs and stuff them in their mouths to stifle their cries. They discovered that the sweet flavour not only offset the pain but was something new in the way of sweetmeats when these were few in the land.

Beatings became highly popular and the liquorice twigs were soon worn out, but fragments which had been swept out of the school into the garden took root and flourished exceedingly in the soil of Pontefract. Soon the liquorice crop became a local industry with a bye-law to forbid growers to sell or give away roots. "Pontefract cakes" acquired a world-wide fame but the only link with the schoolmaster's find was in the by-name of "Spanish" which Yorkshire children often called the long strips of black liquorice.

Sporting Curate

THE village of Dore, now part of Sheffield, was once noted for its variety of trades. There were button-makers, boot and shoemakers, clock makers and saw makers, as well as (with the neighbouring Totley) eighteen tailors making stays and quilted petticoats for the ladies. There were also some remarkable curates about one of whom, in the days when hounds hunted the district, this story is told. One Sunday afternoon, when the service was in full swing, the hounds passed the old chapel which then existed where Dore church now stands. Instantly the congregation all rose to witness the passing hunt and indeed to follow the dogs, when the voice of their curate stopped them. Hurrying down from the pulpit he cried: "Now my friends, we will all start together."

3 The Plain of York

He Went Too Fast

PART true, part legend is the story of Lumley Kettlewell, who believed in fasting. He wanted to persuade the world to go without food altogether. Kettlewell was the son of a prosperous Yorkshire farmer who lived at Bolton Percy at the end of the 18th century. He might have lived a comfortable life but for a belief that came to him as a young man that eating was one of the world's biggest blunders. He set out to cure the world but began with himself, or rather with his horse, thus anticipating the modern method of trying it on the dog. He began gradually to eradicate the horse's habit of eating, as one would aim at curing the smoking habit. Slowly he reduced its diet. But the inevitable end was reached. The horse died. But this did not dismay Lumley Kettlewell. He calmly noted, with regret but not with lost hope, that as soon as the beast grew accustomed to living without food it died.

Next he tried a dog, then a donkey, then a fox. They also died—just when they were getting used to the new life. So Kettlewell—and this is proof at least of the man's sincerity—at last began to practise upon himself. He sacrificed his farm, his furniture and his clothes for his cause. The neighbours jeered and his own relatives expressed themselves freely about his absurd belief. Indomitable will and an iron constitution kept him going on a diet that was steadily reduced to vanishing point, until he too came to the inevitable end of his experiment —death in a York lodging house at the age of 68, martyr to a fantastic theory.

A Queen's Escape

THE battle of Towton Field, near Tadcaster, will always stand in history as one of the most bitter ever fought on English soil. John Richard Green, the historian, said of it that "no such battle had ever been seen in England since the fight of Senlac." It was fought on a fearful day in March in the year 1461, when a snow blizzard raged so hard that the soldiers could scarcely distinguish one side from the other. Nearly 120,000 men of the rival Houses of York and Lancaster contended for victory for over six hours in hand-to-hand combat. When at last the Lancastrian force broke in disorder

the little stream that flowed through the field became a river of blood, and a Yorkist officer counted more than 20,000 Lancastrian corpses on the field. The battle marked the end of the reign of the House of Lancaster and of the unhappy King Henry and his Queen Margaret, who were harried by pursuing troops and forced to fly to Scotland. And thereby hangs a legend:

It was on a still spring evening, soon after the Battle of Towton, that Athelstan, the kindly Abbot of Egglestone Abbey on the banks of the Tees, sat hoping for news of the outcome of the battle. All manner of rumours had floated into the Abbey and there was talk of much terrible fighting, but news travelled slowly in those days, and the Abbot, whose sympathies were with the King, had perforce to exercise patience. While he thus sat, the brother in charge of the Abbey gates approached. "Reverend father," he cried. "There are three wayfarers at the gate craving admittance. They are in desperate straits and seem to be in fear of pursuit."

The Abbot hesitated. It was late and strange visitors had a

way of causing trouble. "What are they like, these strangers?" he asked.

"One is clad in a religious habit, another is but a stripling, and the third is a man at arms," was the reply.

"Let them enter," said the Abbot, "and we will see them." As the three begrimed wayfarers entered the room it was plain to see that although the stripling and the man-at-arms were as the monk had described them, the figure in the religious garb and with closely veiled face was that of a woman. And as the woman threw off her cloak and unveiled her face, the Abbot fell on his knees and reverently kissed her hand. He had been at Court and instantly recognised the fugitive as the former proud Queen Margaret. She bade the old Abbot rise and quickly told him of the Royal defeat at Towton. She explained that she and her son, the stripling, were flying from the Earl of Warwick, the leader of the Yorkist forces, but were now surrounded. She pleaded for his help to get her through the Yorkist lines which surrounded the Abbey.

Even as she spoke there was a mighty thundering at the gates of the Abbey—the pursuers had arrived. Cries of "Death to the Red Rose" could be heard through the thick walls of the great building. The old Abbot did not delay. He sent for a peasant, Walter by name, and whispered to him a few instructions. "Trust this man," he said to the Queen, "He is an old forester, and knows the path through the woods blindfold."

He gave them a hurried blessing and bade them follow the peasant. Walter led them into the church and halted before a pillar. He pressed a spring and at once the solid masonry moved and revealed a dark opening into which the fugitives entered. The stone was only just moved back into place when shouts and cries denoted that the soldiery had entered the church and were searching only a few yards away for the Queen and her son. Lighting a torch, the forester led the way down steps which seemed to descend into the very bowels of the earth. Through long winding passages the party travelled in single file until they came to a barricade of wood and stones bound together with branches of trees.

With the aid of the man-at-arms the forester made a passage through the barricade, and soon the little party found themselves in the open-air well beyond the Yorkist lines. Walter would here have left the party, but the Queen constrained him to guide them further. "Do not leave us," she urged, "you have the hope of England in your keeping. Take us to Bishopdale and we shall be in safety."

The peasant was moved by her plea. He led them to a village near by, secured food and horses and did not leave them until the Queen and her son were in safe company. Alas for the Queen's hopes, her son never became King. She managed to escape with her husband to France and raised an army to defeat the Yorkists. But 10 years after her escape she was defeated at Tewkesbury and taken captive, her son was stabbed, and Henry, her husband, died in the Tower. It was the end of the House of Lancaster.

The Book of Fate

IN a tiny deserted cobbler's shop which lay in the very shadows of York Minster a woebegone man was sobbing bitterly and loudly, so loudly in fact that a worthy knight who was passing stopped his horse by the door of the shop and enquired the reason for the tears. "Alack," said the man gloomily, "may Providence forgive me, but I have already five children and know not how to provide for them, and now my wife has just given birth to another daughter."

The knight proved sympathetic and, having some ability as a seer, drew his Book of Fate from his saddle bow and declared he would foretell the child's future. Great was the astonishment of the poor cobbler when the knight grew plainly agitated at what he saw in the book, and still greater was his amazement when the knight turned to him and offered to adopt the newly-arrived infant as his own, promising to make the child heir to his possessions. Sorely distressed at this turn of events but thinking of no better answer, the cobbler consented, and in a few moments the knight was cantering away with the strange burden of a newly-born child under his arm. Not until he was out of sight of the city did he stop, and as he rode he turned over in his mind the prophecy of his book that this child was destined to marry his only son.

This he determined with many oaths should not happen, and he spurred his horse till he came to a deserted place by the bank of the river Ouse. Here he dismounted and flung the infant into the middle of the river and with a last oath rode away, rejoicing that he had triumphed over the plans of destiny. Had he stayed a little longer he might have seen the helpless little bundle washed up on the shore and watched its discovery by an old fisherman who bore it away tenderly to his cottage.

Some 15 years later the knight was riding with some friends along the banks of the Ouse when they were attracted by a beautiful girl who stood at the door of a fisherman's cottage. They stopped to purchase some fish, and as they bought they marvelled at the graciousness and sweetness of the maid. Even as they rode away they could not forbear to discuss her charms, and as a contribution to the discussion the old knight said that he would look in his Book of Fate to see which of his love-sick friends would marry the maiden. But he did not tell them the result of the consultation with the book for he realised that here was the child he had flung into the stream long before, and that his own son was still destined to be the husband of this girl.

Once more he attempted to prevent the workings of the Book of Fate. Sending to the cottage for the old fisherman who was acting as the girl's guardian, the knight urged that he allow the girl to carry a message from him to his brother, who was a noble knight living in Scarborough. And after some persuasion the fisherman agreed. It was not long before the girl was on her way, bearing in her purse the message of the knight and with a goodly sum of money to assist her on the road. After travelling many miles she came to an inn where she was provided with a room and a comfortable bed on which she soon fell into a sound sleep after the weariness of her journey. Now it chanced that a thief prowled round the inn that night and eventually found access to the room where the girl slept. Her purse lay on the table and as the thief emptied it he discovered the sealed message: "Dear brother—the bearer of this note is a doer of mischief. Put her to death immediately."

Whether it was a lash of compassion on the part of the thief, or the thought that one good turn deserved another, will never be known, but the fact remains that he altered the note to read: "Dear brother—the bearer of this note has all the virtues. Marry her to my son." Next day the girl arose early and continued her journey to Scarborough. When the knight had read the note he presented the maiden to his nephew and the two fell in love at first sight. The news of the wedding, however, reached the bridegroom's father and he set off for Scarborough in great rage to seek an explanation. As he rode into the town he met his new daughter-in-law and repeated his exploit of many years before by carrying her off to a lonely place on the seashore. Here he would have killed her had she not begged so hard for mercy and promised to obey any command.

Relenting, he took a gold ring from her finger, flung it out to the waves and made the girl swear that until she saw the ring again and placed it on her finger she would neither see him nor his son. And he left her weeping bitterly, not knowing how to earn a living in that desolate part of the country. As she wandered weary and hungry down the lanes that led away from the sea, she met the retainer of a nobleman's house who was in great trouble because the cook had been taken ill and there was no-one to fill the place. The girl volunteered and soon found that she was a favourite of all at the castle. A few weeks later a great banquet was given by the nobleman and many guests were invited. As she looked through the castle window to see the flowing garments and the gay clothes of the men, the new cooking maid—still sorrowful at heart— was astonished to see the knight and his son arrive.

While she was torn between joy and misery she chanced to cut open a fish that was to be prepared for the table and she noticed something sparkle inside its body. It was the knight's ring, thus restored to the very castle where the knight was staying. When the feast was over, as was the custom in those days, the cooking maids and chief servants were called to the banqueting hall and praised for their dishes. It was then that the nobleman pointed out the strange girl who had come to take the place of the indisposed cook. No sooner had the knight set eyes on her than he drew his sword, rushed at her and would have killed her had she not raised her hand on which was the sparkling ring. After the failure of the third attempt to thwart the Book of Fate, the knight acknowledged that he could no longer battle against the course of destiny. He gave the young couple his blessing, and in the best phrase of all fairy stories "they lived happily ever after."

Transformation Scene

THE river Wharfe has a reputation for rising and falling rapidly. One day it is almost dry and the next day in flood. It was this peculiarity which was responsible for the reputed verses by Dr. Eades, one time Dean of Winchester, who crossed the river at Tadcaster one summer, on his way to Durham. He wrote:

The muse in Tadcaster can find no theme,
But a noble bridge without a stream.

He returned that way in the middle of winter—and added two more lines:

The verse before on Tadcaster was just,
But now great floods we see, and dirt for dust.

Mother, Nurse and Child

A CENTURY ago, in 1869, a reputable clergyman wrote to Mr. Baring-Gould to tell him of an odd apparition which appeared at Trinity Church, Micklegate, York.

The clergyman had attended a service at the church one

August Sunday morning and sat in the gallery facing the east window, which was of stained glass except for a border of unstained glass all round the window. Before the service began, and then many times during the morning, ghostly figures outside the church moved across the window. They appeared to be two women and a child. One, presumably the mother, came first and then beckoned to the others. The child accompanied by the other woman, possibly the child's nurse, then appeared, and the mother caressed it, seemed greatly distressed, made frantic gestures of despair, and eventually all three figures moved away. This apparition was apparently seen at various times by many people, sometimes vaguely through the stained glass and at other times clearly through the clear glass border. Usually the women were in white, with the features veiled. One account said that the mother's grief was intensified when a hymn was played loudly on the organ. Sunday school children who sat in the gallery were so familiar with the figures that they referred to them as "Mother, nurse and child."

There was nothing in the graveyard outside the church to create the strange drama. Indeed one rector who wanted to get rid of the apparition notion had some trees felled so that their reflection on the glass could not create an illusion of figures. But the apparations continued to appear. So the legend grew that they were the ghosts of a York family—father, mother and only child—who had lived nearby many years before. When the plague broke out in the city it carried off the child and, as was the custom, its body was buried outside the city walls to avoid the spread of infection. The child's parents were buried in a grave in the churchyard near the east window. So the ghostly nurse brought the child back from its plague pit to the grave of its parents to the mingled joy and distress of the mother.

Jovial Archbishop

ONE of the merriest archbishops of York was surely Henry Bowett, the 49th holder of the office, who was translated from

the Bishopric of Bath and Wells in 1405 and died in 1423. He preferred his palace at Otley to that at York, and claret to any other drink. He was reputed to consume with congenial friends fourscore tuns of claret each year (a tun was 252 wine gallons) and one of his earliest tasks was to enlarge the palace kitchens. Of him, or someone very like him, a poet wrote:

The poet Praed's immortal Vicar
Who wisely wore the cleric gown;
Sound in theology and in liquor
Quite human, though a true divine.
His fellow men he would not libel
He gave his friends good, honest wine
And drew his doctrine from the Bible.

The tomb of this jovial man is seen in York Minster.

Raising the Dust

FOSTON, some eight miles from York, is widely known as the parish to which Sydney Smith, the witty Canon and Edinburgh Reviewer, was "exiled" by Archbishop Harcourt when he put into force the Clergy Residence Act of 1803 compelling absent clerics, known as "galloping parsons," to reside in their parishes. The church, like the pulpit, had long been neglected when Sydney Smith arrived. He recorded: "When I began to thump the cushion of my pulpit on first coming to Foston, as is my wont when I preach, the accumulated dust of 150 years made such a cloud that for some minutes I lost sight of my congregation". The dust has gone, the pulpit has been rebuilt, and now the church contains a monumental tablet to its famous parson.

New Eyes for Old

THERE is nothing new under the sun, even to the transplanting of eyes, now a commonplace of surgical science. St. John of Beverley earned the reputation of curing a man of blindness. More than 400 years later St. William of York went even further, according to legend. The story is told in a petition to the Pope in 1226 for the canonization of the former Archbishop of York.

A knight named Ralph was accused of breaking the King's peace and by the knightly code he was put to trial by conflict with another knight named Besing. After a long and fierce duel Ralph was overcome because one of his eyes was put out. This was evidence of his guilt and he was therefore condemned to be deprived of the other eye. This was done by the executioner. Ralph, without sight and feeling he had been unjustly punished, spent many days in prayer and fasting and eventually found his way to the tomb of the Blessed William. There, says the legend, two eyes were given him—smaller and of different colour to those he had lost—but sound enough to provide him with sharp and clear sight.

Fame from an Apple

YORKSHIRE has many great houses famous for their historic associations, or their art treasures, but only one famous because of an apple. Ribston Hall, not far from Goldsborough between Knaresborough and York, had the distinction of propagating the first Ribston pippin. A member of the Goodricke family, which resided there at the turn of the 18th century, received three pips from a friend in Rouen in Normandy. All three were planted in the Ribston Hall gardens. Two died but the third flourished, and from that survivor came the modern stock of Ribston pippins.

Kirkham Abbey

KIRKHAM Abbey, on the banks of the Derwent, owed its foundation to a fatal hunting accident, according to an oft-told story. Walter l'Espec's son—another Walter—was fond of the chase and one day as he rode at a breakneck speed through the woods he was thrown violently from his horse and broke his neck. When the elder Walter and his wife Adeline were told of the boy's death they grieved bitterly. To distract them from their grief and bring consolation, a kinsman urged them to build and endow a religious house at Kirkham, and so the priory came into being with the kinsman, William l'Espec, as the first prior. At the Dissolution of the monasteries it had 17 inmates. Now little remains but a beautiful gateway and portions of the chancel walls.

A more recent and more cheerful event was the Kirkham bird fair. At midnight each Trinity Sunday it was the custom for the youths and maidens of Kirkham village to meet on the bridge over the Derwent and there exchange their pet birds. An unlikely excuse, no doubt, but the merry-making and drinking which followed went on until the sun set on the Monday evening.

Battle in the Skell

ROBIN Hood must have been a thirsty soul judging by the number of wells named after him. Many have a legend about the outlaw and one of the most famous is at Fountains on the river Skell where Robin had his encounter with the Curtal Friar. Legend says that Robin Hood was so pleased with the archery of Little John that he doubted whether he could find his match even though he travelled 100 miles. His companion, Will Scadlock, was very scornful and declared:

There lives a Curtal Friar in Fountains Abbey
Will beate both him and thee.

So Robin Hood set off to search for this rival in the country round Ripon and in a glade by the Skell he came upon the friar. At once he exerted his authority as an outlaw of the woods:

Carry me over this water, thou Curtal Friar
Or else thy life's forlorne.

The friar obeyed and took him across the river without a word. Then he turned to the outlaw and commanded:

Carry me over this water, thou fine fellow
Or it shall breede thee paine.

So Robin did as he was told but then insisted that the friar must carry him back again. This time the friar dropped him in mid-stream, and they at once began to fight (which is probably what they had both hankered after). Legend says

that they fought long and fiercely in the river and on the land until Robin, finding himself worsted, a little unfairly "blew blasts three" on his horn and 50 followers rushed from the woods to his aid. The friar retorted by "whistling whistles three" and 50 dogs rushed to help their master. The fight continued until Little John appeared with his bow and shot many of the dogs dead, upon which the Curtal Friar gave in and became a member of Robin Hood's company. But what happened about the archery contest and how the well came into the picture the story does not tell.

Little John appears in another story of the outlaw in Yorkshire; this time when Robin Hood was dying, and the scene was the ancient nunnery of Kirklees in the Calder valley. Near this nunnery, now only a site, Robin Hood was taken grievously ill and remembered that the Abbess was a kinswoman of his. He sought rest and refuge at the nunnery and the Abbess admitted him, bled him for his ailment, and then left him in a locked room to bleed to death. After a great effort he managed to escape through the window and for the last time blew three feeble blasts on his horn. Little John heard the horn and arrived only to find Robin at the point of death. Fitting an arrow to his bow the outlaw shot the arrow into the air, saying:

Where this arrow is taken up
There shall my grave digged be.
Lay a green sod under my head
And another at my feet;
And lay my bent bow by my side,
Which was my music sweet.

Ripon's Curfew

RIPON is one of the few cities in England to retain its curfew in full ceremonial. Just before nine o'clock each night the Sergeant at Mace clad, as someone has described it, like a "dismounted highwayman" walks out into the Market Place and stands listening, all unconscious of the little crowd which gathers round him. So soon as the cathedral clock has ceased to strike, the horn-blower comes to life. He lifts the curved horn which he wears on a strap round his shoulders, blows into it, and produces the most mournful sound as a result. It is a cross between a wail and a sigh and lasts for the best part of a minute. The same performance is repeated to the same audience at each of the four corners of the Market Place and then three times in front of the house of the current Mayor. Then the horn-blower goes home.

A variation of this ceremony was responsible for the strange event which occurred some years ago. The Mayor of the year thought it would be a suitable tribute to the memory of Hugh Ripley, the last Wakeman and the fore-runner of the present Mayors, whose uncomfortable monument is in the nave of the Minster, if the horn was blown once more before the Wakeman's house. Being a very special occasion the loyal audience this night became a considerable crowd. The horn was blown, but before the moan of it had died away there was a stir among the spectators. A face, declared to be that of Hugh Ripley, had appeared at the upper window of the Wakeman's house. There was great excitement and much heated argument. Could it have been a hoax? Or could it have been the ghost of the worthy Wakeman? Keys were sent for and the house, which was uninhabited, was searched, but no living soul was found. Thus was another story added to Ripon's already picturesque history.

Nemesis

A CRIME story with a difference is told about the gibbet stone in Sawley Lane not far from Ripon. A man and a girl often met in secret in Hebden Wood close by and all went well until she discovered she was pregnant. His affection cooled and there were frequent quarrels. Then one night screams were heard and the couple were not seen again. Some time later newly-turned soil revealed the place where the murdered woman and her unborn twins had been buried, and the news of the crime spread widely.

The scene now moves to a port somewhere overseas where a man walked into a harbour-side bar, bought drinks all round and called for a toast: "To the ewe and two lambs buried in Hebden Wood." It meant little to most of the company except for two men recently arrived from England who by chance had heard of the murder. The police were told, the man was arrested and brought back to Yorkshire. The story ends in an unlikely way for it is said that the murderer was punished by being chained to this gibbet stone and that he remained there for many weeks until he died of insanity. It is more likely that he was hanged there on a gibbet as was the custom.

4 East Yorkshire

Poetic Landlord

ALEXANDER Mackintosh was landlord of the *Red Lion Inn* at Driffield, a sportsman, and a poet. His hostelry was famed as a meeting place for owners of greyhounds and other dogs, for anglers and for those interested in "hunting, hawking coursing and other field sports." He wrote a book, published in 1810, entitled *The Driffield Angler*, which included instructions on shooting,

the manner of killing deer and the training of greyhounds, and it ran to several editions. In it he immortalised Snowball, a greyhound of legendary fame, owned by a certain major of Topham:

The outstretched Wolds where glory won,
In many a nobler course, her speed
Snowball resigns unto her breed
Hung round with trophies of her praise
The prizes of her youthful days.

He also recorded in his book two almost legendary pike, one caught at Driffield weighing 28 lb. and another at Rise weighing 38 lb.

Sanctuary at Beverley

THE right of sanctuary from private revenge or the severities of the law has been recognised from the very earliest times. In Biblical records there is evidence of the existence of cities of refuge. Greeks and Romans alike had their sacred places where the fugitive could find at least a temporary respite from his pursuers. Very early in Christian history the custom of allowing Christian churches to offer protection to those fleeing from justice came into existence, and an important part of the duty of the clergy was that of acting as intermediaries between criminals and the officers of justice.

Under a code of laws drawn up by Alfred the Great, church "frith" or sanctuary was recognised, and sanctuary seekers were protected for seven days, or under certain circumstances for 30 days. Occasionally it happened that the sanctuary right was violated, and the penalty for such violation was very severe. The most notable case of sacrilege of this sort was, of course, the murder of Thomas a' Becket at the Altar of St. Benedict in his own cathedral church of Canterbury. Among the oldest and most important of all the sanctuary rights throughout the kingdom were those pertaining to Beverley and its Minster.

In honour of St. John of Beverley privileges were granted by King Athelstan in the year 937 and continued for over 500 years. By these the rights of sanctuary existed in the distance of one league, or about a mile and a half from the Minster in every direction. Within this great sanctuary circle were other boundaries coming closer to the Minster. The third of these began at the entrance to the churchyard, the fourth at the nave door, the fifth at the choir screen, and the sixth and last at the actual high altar and Frith Stool which stood close by. For violating these various bounds the penalties grew increasingly great as they approached the Minster, varying from a fine of eight pounds at the outer boundary to the forfeit of life for any sacrilege at the high altar.

How strong was the general belief in the "divine rights of sanctuary" is shown in a story told by Alfred, a priest of the Minster, in the reign of Henry I: At the time when William the Conqueror was "Wasting the North" in revenge for rebellion against his rule, his troops were stationed near Beverley and as a result the local people fled to the church for protection. Some of the soldiers decided to raid the church for plunder, and led by one Toustain on horseback they entered the church. But no sooner had Toustain crossed the threshold than his horse stumbled, and Toustain fell with his neck broken and hands distorted like those of a mis-shapen monster. The soldiers fled in fear at the sight and even the Conqueror was dismayed when told the story, so that he confirmed all the privileges of the church, gave it a grant of lands at Sigglesthorne, and decreed that the laws of the blessed Saint John should be everywhere spared from the "Wasting."

The Frith Stool was a wide stone chair, once probably inscribed, but now with all trace of lettering defaced. The chair, which may date from the time of Athelstan himself, was the goal of pursued men for many miles around, and if stones could speak it could relate many dramatic stories of those who had committed some grave wrong finding refuge there from the hand of the law or the fury of revengeful relatives. From as far away as Norfolk, Devon, Lancaster, and Cumberland fugitives fled to Beverley, racing against their pursuers, to throw themselves at the mercy of the Church.

Those who had committed murder, theft or other crimes, on coming within the bounds were received there by officials of the church and allowed to stay for 30 days and nights within the precincts of the Minster. Food and accommodation were provided, and during the time of their stay it was the duty of the canons to endeavour to obtain peace and pardon for the fugitives. If these efforts failed, then at the end of the 30 days the offender was taken to the outer boundary and handed over to the coroner who had then to offer the fugitive the choice of taking his trial or being outlawed from the realm. In the latter case the fugitive was given a fixed time in which to reach a named port from where he was conveyed overseas, never to return.

Beverley, however, had a third alternative—in which it differed from most other ecclesiastical sanctuaries. This was the right of the criminal to take an oath swearing to become a servant of the church and to live within the town of Beverley for the rest of the fugitive's life. Those who accepted this method were known as Frithmen. A Frithman had to surrender to the Crown all his possessions either in land or money, but was allowed to live anywhere within the area of immunity, and to follow his own craft and trade. He could not become a burgess but could hold office in his trade guild, and there is evidence that many became very prosperous. In common with many other ecclesiastical rights, the special sanctuary privileges of Beverley were swept away by Henry

VIII, about 1540, and despite many attempts to restore it the same all-embracing liberty never returned to the church.

Beachcomber

THE nickname of one Thomas Smith who lived at South Ferriby was "Coin Tommy." His hobby was "beachcombing" along the banks of the Humber and he made a speciality of metal objects washed up by the tides. He stuffed his pockets

with everything he found, without bothering to examine his hoard, and when he returned home he piled it all into an immense number of old tin boxes, which he never looked at again. Strange stories spread about his collection, but he was uninterested and still went on gathering. When he died his store was opened up and his treasures brought buyers from all parts of the country, for his "beat" had included the site of a Roman cemetery which the tides regularly uncovered. So he had a wonderful gathering of brooches, rings, bracelets and other valuable ornaments which originally belonged to the Roman community at Peruaria where the Roman Road crossed the Humber. Among it all were over 3,000 Roman coins.

Lost Links

HEDON in the East Riding was an important town with a charter, a mayor, and aldermen when Hull was only a fishing village. According to legend it also had a magnificent mayoral chain made of links of pure gold, some fifty of them altogether. Alas, as the years went by the chain became shorter and eventually disappeared altogether. Then it was discovered that each retiring mayor, on handing it over to his successor, had carefully removed a link as a memento of his year of office. It must have been an uncomfortably short chain as the fifty years drew to a close.

Cupid's Well

NEAR Keyingham, the East Riding village which stands on a ridge with Hull on one side and Patrington on the other, there used to be a "pilgrim's cross" and near it was a well, both known as St. Philip's. The well had great popularity among young ladies. A lovely maiden would beguile a young man to the well and with him gaze into it to see their joint reflection. At the moment they saw it she would throw in a silver coin, and the young man was as good as engaged. After all, there were fairies at the bottom of that well and the silver coin was their reward for doing the rest.

Great and Small

A GIANT and a dwarf were both produced in the East Riding. The giant was William Bradley, born at Market Weighton in 1787 and one of thirteen children all except himself who were of normal porportions and normal sized parents. There can be no doubt of his claim to fame for at the age of eleven he weighed 11 stones and before he was twenty he topped 27 stones. It is recorded that his shoes were 15 inches long and 5½ inches broad, his stockings 3 ft. 9 in. from top to toe, and his walking stick 49 in. long. He lived a normal life working on his father's farm on the Wolds, was a moderate eater and drank nothing stronger than tea. Later he found it profitable to appear at exhibitions as "The Yorkshire Giant." He died at the age of 33 and was buried in Market Weighton church.

Little more than twenty years later and at Shipton only a few miles away was born Edwin Calvert, who never grew bigger than 36 in. in height. Alas, he failed to follow his predecessor's example for he became a heavy drinker and died in 1859 at the age of 17.

5 Cleveland and the Coast

Sarkless Kitty

A RATHER macabre little story comes from the pleasant hollow of Farndale. Kitty was a girl who fell in love with a wealthy farmer's son and hoped that he would marry her. But when he found out she was expecting a baby he disclaimed responsibility and refused to have any more to do with her. Much pleading and many tears followed until he agreed to meet her once more at an appointed place in the dale to renew their love. A fearful storm struck the valley that night however. There was a cloudburst on the moors and the little river Dove became a fierce torrent. Kitty waited long for her lover but he did not appear and a farm man told her he had seen a horseman riding hell-for-leather towards Kirkbymoorside at the height of the storm.

Convinced now that she was not only betrayed but deserted, the distraught girl tore off all her clothes—"sark (chemise) and all" in the local phrase—and plunged into the raging waters of the Dove. A few days later when the water abated her body was discovered by the ford, and close to it the body of her drowned lover with the new wedding ring in his pocket he had bought for her at Kirkbymoorside before he was caught by the storm-filled river. Both bodies were buried in the churchyard, hers at the crossroads as she was a "suicide."

There was a stranger sequel. The ghost of Sarkless Kitty haunted the ford, weird laughter was heard and her spectral shape was seen each year as the river claimed another victim on the anniversary of her death. How long this fearful haunting would have continued no-one could guess, but it greatly troubled the local people in the dale. Among them was an old Farndale Quaker who thought so much about it that one night he had a vivid dream. Waking his wife he told her of his vision and together in pitch darkness they went to the

Church Houses, Farndale

crossroads, disinterred the remains of Sarkless Kitty and re-buried her in an old Quaker graveyard nearby. From that time the ghost of Sarkless Kitty was never seen again and the toll of deaths ended. The dalesfolk were pleased but puzzled. Only the old Quaker and his wife knew that at last she was at peace by her lover.

The Hole of Horcum

THE great hollow known as the Hole of Horcum, which lies alongside the Pickering to Whitby road, was called in stage-coach days the Devil's Punch Bowl, but that may have derived from the bowls of punch brewed at the nearby inn. Certainly the Devil has always been associated with the hole, as evidenced by two legends. One was that he scooped up a handful of earth to throw at his wife, and that the marks of his fingers can still be seen on the side of the hole. The credulous can still see his thumb-print. The other is that the Devil, in league with the giant Horcum, between them scooped up enough soil and rock to make the cone-shaped Blakey Topping, which can be seen not far away.

Earth-moving seemed a popular occupation then as now, for another legend relates that a giant and his wife built both

Mulgrave Castle and Pickering Castle, many miles apart, from local stone, and that they had only a hammer between them. When one or other wanted the hammer—or more stones—they called to each other and threw the wanted requirements to each other. Somewhere on the Pickering-Whitby road there are still some large stones which fell short.

Farmers' Lament

A NOT uncommon complaint by Yorkshire farmers is "two days wet to one day fine." It was enshrined as a saying in verse many years ago, the authorship being variously attributed but from its spelling probably a Cleveland man. It was entitled a "Yorkshire Farmers' Lament on the Harvest of 1800." Part of the poem runs as follows:

It rains agean, ah dear declare
It's twea days wet, to ya day fair
Syke tarms as theers, was nivver seen
Us farmers will be beggared clean
An' wot a mess o' mouldy hay
An' taties rotting all away,
An' harvest fookes' wages ganin on
An' there they stant can't de a ton (*turn*)
Times is se bad, aa's very flaid
Rents, rates and taxes 'll nivver git paid.

Whoops-a-Daisy

YORKSHIRE folk know many ways of curing whooping cough—or "kin-cough" as it was commonly known. They would pass the ailing child several times under a donkey, or go to live near a gasworks, or visit the Hob Thrush who had his home at Runswick Bay. A mother of an ailing child would take the sufferer to find the Hob Hole, a place still marked on the map although the cavern which gave it its name seems to have vanished. There she addressed the Hob Thrush, who dwelt inside:

Hob-hole Hob
My bairn's gotten t'kin-cough
Tak't off. Tak't off.

After that the child could enjoy a holiday all the better.

Fairy in a Tantrum

THOSE who think of fairies as light, winsome and gentle of form and manner might ponder on a certain fairy named

Jeanie, who lived in a secluded bower deep in the woods of Mulgrave, near Whitby. She lived there very happily with fairy-like tasks (whatever they might be), and pursuing an untroubled life until a local farmer's son heard of her and, being a curious young man to say the least, sought out her hiding place and even called out her name. Her blissful solitude invaded, she became incensed with rage and rushed out at him, wand in hand. The young farmer proved more curious than he was bold. He turned and fled on his horse with the fairy in hot pursuit. He feared an awful fate but remembered that fairies can never cross water. So he set his horse at a stream just as she struck him with her wand. He returned home, horseless and on foot.

The Penny Hedge

THE planting of the Norngarth or Penny Hedge at Whitby is an annual ritual which always attracts a goodly company of spectators, although not all who watch know of its significance. Legend assigns its origin to a strange happening in the district in the reign of Henry II. Three gentlemen were out hunting a wild boar and followed its trail to the home of the Hermit of Eskdaleside where it found refuge with the holy man. The three hunters forgot they were gentlemen and because the hermit tried to bar their way they man-handled him so roughly that he was on the point of death.

Remorse overtook them and they begged his forgiveness which, before he died, he gave on certain conditions: that on the Eve of Ascension they should go to the wood of Eskdaleside, take ten stakes, ten stowers and ten yedders, to be cut with a penny knife, go to Whitby harbour before 9 a.m. and build at the water's brim a hedge which must stand three tides before being washed away. On the completion of the task the Officer of Eskdaleside was to blow his horn and cry, "Out on ye, out on ye." Failure to fulfil the conditions would entail the forfeiture of the culprits' lands to the Abbot of Whitby. What happened to the boar neither legend nor tradition relates.

Vision at Whitby

ALTHOUGH Whitby Abbey was founded and endowed by Osway, King of the Northumbrians, and was dedicated to St. Peter, the monastery was always ascribed to St. Hilda, who was so highly venerated that many miracles were attributed to her and have become legend. But there is one legend about Hilda herself as related by a Whitby historian in 1776 as follows:

"At a particular time of the year, viz., in the summer months, the sunbeams fall in the inside of the northern part of the choir, and 'tis then that the spectators who stand on the west side of Whitby churchyard, so as just to see the most northerly part of the abbey, past the north of Whitby church, imagine they perceive in one of the highest windows there the resemblance of a woman arranged in a shroud. Though we are certain this is only a reflection caused by the splendour of the sun's beams, yet report says, and it is constantly believed among the vulgar, to be an appearance of Lady Hilda, in her shroud or rather in her glorified state."

I Shot an Arrow

WHEN Robin Hood and Little John were roaming the countryside they were given hospitality one night at Whitby Abbey—after all Robin Hood's Bay is only just round the corner. As usual they boasted of their prowess as archers and so impressed the Abbot that next morning he invited them both to the top of the tower to see who could shoot an arrow the greatest distance. They did as his bidding and shot their arrows in the direction of Whitby Laithes. Legend does not tell who won but the monks marked the distance where the two arrows fell by erecting pillars to mark the places—two miles from the Abbey tower.

Tale of a Tithe

THERE are many legends of Flamborough for the community living there was more self-contained and kept its speech, customs and stories longer than almost any other part of Yorkshire. They will tell you today how schoolchildren ran round a hollow by the roadside in the belief that if they did it nine times a legendary Jenny Lind, who died there, would repeat this rhyme:

Ah'll put on mi bonnet
An' tee on mi shoe,
An' if thoo's not off
Ah'll be efter thoo.

For many centuries Flamborough's fishing industry had to pay a tithe to the Prior of Bridlington all because this right of "scist-fish" was granted to him by Edward III. According to legend the prior was expected to provide flagons of ale and sixpences for the fishermen of Flamborough. Skippers were to be given more but they had to swear a new oath each year to maintain the tithe. No-one knew much about these legendary rights, and the payment of the annual tithe became more burdensome than the ale was worth. So about 200 years ago a worthy native, John Ogle, set out for London to clear up the mystery and have the tithe charge rescinded. Alas, John Ogle died of Black Fever before he could complete the task, so a group of Flamborough men sailed off to London to bring back his body in gratitude for his effort. It was buried in Flamborough and not long afterwards the tithe was lifted forever.

Robin Lythe

THE cliffs of Flamborough have attracted almost as many legends as visitors. One concerns a cavern in the great headland which has two entrances —one from the sea and the other from the land—and known as Robin Lythe's Hole. But who was Robin Lythe? Some say he was a pirate who raided passing merchant coasters and then retreated with his plunder to this cavern which was his headquarters—like a spider hiding in his web but always ready to pounce. Less romantically, it is said he was a forlorn mariner shipwrecked off Flamborough Head, who was washed ashore into the cavern and so survived. You can take your choice.

Bellman's Cry

DICKY Fletcher was Bellman of Bridlington and an octogenarian. He might have reached his century for he was an active and vigorous man, had he not fallen down the cellar steps in 1827. All his announcements were made in local dialect thus:

Tak'n oop this foornoon, opud th'nooarth sans,
Two keis, which I hev in mi hans
Who-iver hes lost 'em mun just cum to mea
An'they sal hev 'em agean, an we agreea.

Two Sisters of Withernsea

IN a number of north-country parishes you will be told the story of two sisters who each wished to build a new church for the parish but one wanted a spire and the other a tower, so now you will find both a spire and a tower in the same parish. At Withernsea there is the same legend—with a difference. Here two churches were built, one with a tower and the other with a spire. But the sisters forgot the sea. Since the Norman Conquest the coast has been eaten away by the sea at least one mile. So first went the church with the spire and then the church with the tower. And not only the churches but the gravestones of the two sisters eventually went the same way.

Humber Enterprise

THERE are many stories to explain how Ravenspurn, once a port at the mouth of the Humber where kings landed, vanished into the sea and is now a lost town. Fewer know the story of two other now vanished ports nearby, Old Ravenser and Ravenser Odd. "Ald Ravenser" was a place of some importance until about 1234 when a ship was wrecked on a nearby sandbank and abandoned. An enterprising man with an eye to the main chance took over the hull and began to sell its contents and later food and drink to passing vessels and local seamen. One or two other folk came to live near this useful shop, ships called there, and Ravenser Odd became a port as "Ald Ravenser" declined. Now, both have gone.

6 A Miscellany

As Clear as Mud

EVER since a West Riding man gave evidence in court that he admitted having possession of a stolen article but had "got shut of it," legal men have found it a difficult task to pin down Yorkshire witnesses to conclusive facts. There is a legendary story still told in places where men of law meet of the questioning of a Yorkshire labourer which went something like this:

Did you see the defendant throw the stone?

I saw a stone and I'm pretty sure t'defendant throwed it.

Was it a large stone?—It were a largish stone.

What was its size?—It were a sizeable stone.

Can you say how big it was?—It were a stone of some bigness.

Can you not tell the jury more about it?—Why, it were something of a stone.

Can you compare it to some other object?—Why, if I were to compare it I reckon as how it were as large as a lump of chalk.

Satan As Stone Mason

FOR a people not prone to shudder much at "ghosts and goulies and things that go bump in the night," Yorkshire folk have a wholesome respect of Satan. They do not blench at his mention or go out of their way to placate him, but they do recognise that he is a fellow of parts, able to get his own way and not the sort to be trifled with. Why Satan should have built so many bridges in Yorkshire and flung so many stones about is as great a mystery as why so many Yorkshire castles should be attributed to giants. But whenever our ancestors were puzzled over the origin of any artificial river crossing they promptly blamed the Devil. One of the finest examples of his handiwork is just outside the county at Kirkby Lonsdale, in Westmorland, but this Devil's Bridge spanning the Lune on the old road from Kendal into Yorkshire is a fine introduction to a stretch of England where the Satanic stone mason has been unusually busy. Indeed where the Devil has proved so helpful a companion to road travellers it is not surprising to find him regarded as not such a bad fellow after all!

An example of his benefaction may be found at the Devil's Bridge near Burnsall, in Wharfedale. Polite people have tried to name this Dibble Bridge, because it spans a small stream called the Dibb, but they are craven folk who will not give the Devil his due. The story goes that when Fountains Abbey was in its prime, a shoemaker and small tenant of part of the Abbey lands, named Ralph Calvert, resided at Thorpe-sub-Montem and journeyed twice a year along this road to pay his rent to the Abbot, dispose of the fruits of his six months' handiwork and return the shoes entrusted to him on his previous visit for repair. He would bring back with him on his return a bag well filled with others that needed attention.

The night before setting out on one of these occasions he had a fearful dream, in which he struggled with the Devil, who in this wild, rocky ravine amid unpleasant surroundings endeavoured to thrust Ralph into a bag similar to the one in which he carried his stock-in-trade. In the morning, however, he started on his journey, and reached the Abbey without ill, assisted at the service, did his business with the Abbot and brethren and then set out with his well-filled bag on his return homewards. When he arrived at the deep ravine, where on previous occasions he had found a small brook which he could easily ford, he now found a mountain torrent through which he could only make his way with difficulty and some danger. After the crossing he sat down to rest and dry his wetted garments, and then as is the way when danger is over he began to wonder at his escape. He could not but recall how exactly it corresponded with the spot seen in his dream.

Trembling fearfully, as well he might, from the cold chill of the stream and the heated thoughts of his brain, the shoemaker fancied he saw the shadow of a man on the road. Then the Devil appeared and a long and not unfriendly conversation ensued in which Satan enquired of the alarmed man if there

Devil's Bridge, Kirkby Lonsdale

was anything that he could do for him. Ralph looked at the swollen torrent and thought of the danger he had lately incurred in crossing it, and of his future journeys that way to the Abbey. So he said: "I have heard that you are a good architect; I wish you would build a bridge across this stream. I know you can do it."

"Yes," replied his visitant, "I can and will do it. At the fourth day from this time come to this spot and you will be astonished. You can bring the whole countryside with you, if you like." The news of Ralph's eerie adventure and of the promise soon spread among the neighbours and he had no small amount of village chaff and ridicule to meet before the eventful Saturday —the fourth day— arrived. But the shoemaker had faith in the Devil. Accompanied by thirty or forty of the villagers he made his way to the dell where, on arrival, they found a beautiful and substantial bridge. In time it fell into so disreputable and dangerous a condition that a very famous native of the parish, Sir William Craven, Lord Mayor of London in the reign of James I, took the matter in hand and built on the old foundations a new bridge which still endures. Men continue to call it the Devil's Bridge.

In Wensleydale in another bridge-building feat, the Devil apparently brought in the giants to assist him as a labouring gang, for in the erection of Kilgrim Bridge near Thornton Steward, stones were required by the Devil from the nearby fells. Even Satan it would seem can tire of good deeds, at least when it involves carrying great boulders half a dozen miles, so the giants were called in to do the fetching and carrying. One of these found his burden too great at East Witton and dropped it where it can be seen to this day.

The bridge itself was only built after the local people had tried in vain over many years to erect a structure strong enough to withstand the heavy floods which came down the river Ure. When at last they gave up the task as a bad job they decided to call in Satan to assist, doubtless because of his Yorkshire reputation as a builder of bridges. He took on the contract on terms, or at least on one term, that the first living creature to cross should be a sacrifice to him.

It was when the bridge was completed and the price had to be paid that the local worthies began to think they had been forced into a bad bargain, but argue as they would the Devil demanded his sacrifice. Then an ancient shepherd had a bright idea. Taking his dog "Grim" down to the river, the old man swam across, struggled out and then whistled for his dog. Disliking the watery way, the dog bounded over the new bridge to his old master—and was promptly whisked away by his new master, the Devil. Thus the name of the bridge became "Kilgrim," and so remains today.

Careless Devil

YORKSHIRE folk have in general taken Shakespeare's advice to "let the Devil be sometimes honoured." Many legends in this book are evidence of this, yet the Devil must have been a pioneer litter-lout in the matter of thrown-away stones. Near Boroughbridge there is a trio of monoliths known as the Devil's Arrows, over the origin of which archaeologists read papers at each other at regular intervals. Some maintain that they are remnants of days of devil-worship, though it seems unlikely that Yorkshire folk would ever go as far as that even with so good-natured a being. Another theory maintains that when Satan disguised as a priest at a

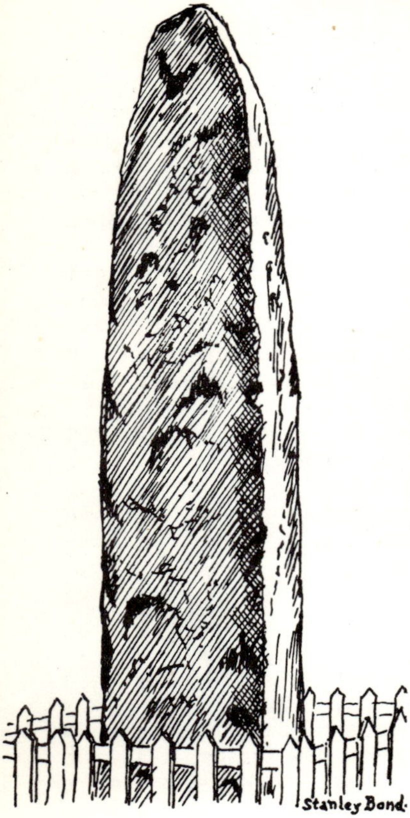

"Marks of the Devil"

Left: The Rudston Monolith, near Bridlington.

Above: The Devil's Arrows, Boroughbridge.

Druid's assembly was uncloaked, he ran away and threw the stones at Aldborough. His aim was faulty.

He is said to have dropped the load of rocks which are now known as Almscliff Crag, while diabolical agency is supposed to account for the tallest monolith in the country at Rudston, near Bridlington. Filey Brigg is the result of Lucifer's grandiose effort to divide the North Sea into two and, as every gold-digger should know, this fallen angel in the guise of a raven, guards a treasure chest in an underground passage in Guisborough Priory. The county has many other Satanic associations. The Devil's Court is on Easby Moor, his Apronful of Stones can be seen on Pockstones Moor, his punchbowl at Saltersgate Moor, and his Elbow on the Pickering-Whitby road.

Night Prowlers

IT has always been a good Yorkshire custom to avoid all truck with lesser demons, whether they were the boggarts which lurked in the caves and potholes in the limestone country, Gabble Ratches which flew overhead in Cleveland and the north, or the Barguest or ghost dog which had many hiding places in the loneliest parts of the country. None of them was the better for knowing and they were best left alone, although now and again they forced themselves on the unwilling attention of honest citizens without invitation. Wordsworth wrote of "Gabriel's Hounds,"

Doomed, with their impious lord, the flying hart
To chase for ever through aerial grounds.

He had probably in mind that same species of creature which moorland folk refer to as Gabble Ratches and describe as "night-birds, whose notes are supposed to be ominous of death." Some held them to be the souls of unbaptised infants, doomed restlessly to flit around their parents' abode. A similar spectre was apparently known by the Danes as *Helrakker*, and was a bird with a huge head and crooked beak. There is a Cleveland legend that an old-time hunting squire on his death-bed ordered all his hounds to be killed and buried at the same time and in the same tomb as himself. These hounds became winged and continued as restless in death as hounds are in life, and were probably the original Gabriel's Hounds.

Boggarts were less intrusive beings and were probably the souls of the departed making the best of uncomfortable surroundings. Haunting limestone clefts, they had a way of howling dismally on windy nights or gurgling ominously at the foot of deep shafts in flood time. They could be seen in churchyards too, if you were careless enough to wander that way at night, and on All Souls' Night they had their own revelries which sensible flesh and blood folk avoided. The ghost dog was a less friendly creature. Of it, Miss Ella Pontefract wrote that at Trollers Gill, in Wharfedale, "the legend of the Barguest carries you back to the time of the Celtic habitation. It says that a shaggy dog-like creature with eyes like saucers haunts this gloomy ravine, and to see it means death unless there is water between you and it."

Gathering Witch Wood

MOST Yorkshire farm folk have believed in the legendary protective powers of witch wood. The Rowan (Mountain Ash) was the favourite witch wood. No owner of livestock when bringing his cattle in from the pastures for the winter months neglected to have in readiness a plentiful supply of it. Pieces were laid in the cow stalls and hung over the door lintels of the farm buildings. There were several observances to be followed very strictly when collecting witch wood. The branches of the rowan tree must be cut off by no other means than a household knife and from a tree that was unknown—trees growing round the farm were familiar to the gatherers and would not do. It must be carried home a different way to the outward journey. To have the full effect it must be gathered on St. Helen's Day. Pieces could be placed at heads of beds, in the dairy, or carried in the trouser pockets.

What's in a Name?

ODDITY of place names is not limited to Yorkshire, but few counties have such strange stories associated with them. "Nonegoby" for example, was a farmhouse at Bramhope near Leeds. It was once an inn and was said to have derived its name from a rhyme coined while the nearby Bramhope railway tunnel was being built:

None go by dry.
If you do the fault's in you
And not in I.

In the Bell Dean Valley in the West Riding is a hamlet known as "Thowt It" on the slopes of Pitty Beck. An old inhabitant explained it thus: "There were nobbut a two-three houses a long way from anywheer else. Folk were that capped when they got there they all said, 'Well, who'd a thowt it.' And t'name stuck."

"Seldom Seen" is a frequent name for farmhouses and usually explains itself, but a row of houses near Cononley in Airedale, known locally as "Frying Pan Cottages," demands a local explanation, which is that many years ago the occupants had only one frying pan between them, so they shared it passing it from cottage to cottage as required.

Even large towns have their stories. Halifax has for long puzzled place-name experts; indeed ever since Camden's original explanation that it was derived from "holy hour" (Old English—halif-feax). His story was that a local maiden long ago refused to please the desires of a lustful priest, so he killed her and hanged her on a tree. Before long the tree became a resort for pilgrims who stripped off the bark as relics and underneath found fibres which they believed were the maiden's holy hair.

There are several "Jumbles Holes" in the West Riding, which may be linked with modern "jumble sales" in that they were usually rough and untidy holes created in hilly country by streams and into which rubbish was jumbled. In the North Riding a farmhouse near Reeth is known as "Dagger Stones," from the site of a legendary "Battle of the Forty Daggers." It sounds a blood-curdling event which, alas, historians have failed to record. There is said to be a dagger-marked stone nearby. "Nunkeeling" in Holderness is probably named from a Benedictine nunnery which was founded there in the 12th century, one of three religious houses in the district, all referred to in the following verse:

If you go to Nunkeeling
You'll find your belly filling
Of whig or of whey.
But go to Swine
Before bedtime
Or else you'll go empty away.
But the Abbot on Meaux
Doth keep a good house
By night and by day.

Notorious Women

YORKSHIRE has no lack of famous men, and much has been written of them, but little is said about the famous women of Yorkshire. Yet they are a remarkable company. Outstanding, in bulk at any rate, was Catherine Haddin, of Huddersfield, who died in 1846 at the age of 34, and weighed 22 stone! She had an exciting life, and was not unknown as a politician in the West Riding. Legend has it that Isabella Cryer, of Leeds, who died in 1774, weighed 40 stone, but there are grave doubts about the accuracy of this figure. The only reliable information is that it took ten men to carry her to her grave.

Most people have heard of Mary Bateman, who was executed at York for a long list of murders and lesser crimes, and whose body was sent to Leeds Infirmary for dissection, portions of her skin being made into souvenirs. But the more worthy Mrs. Isabel Denton, of Beeston, is almost forgotten. Yet she can claim fame for, saddled with a large family and a husband who would not work, she began to make straw hats and bonnets, and is entitled to honour as the inventor of this form of headgear.

Samuel Smiles would have applauded Mrs. Denton and would doubtless have approved of Miss Margaret Wharton of Skelton, near Guisborough, who bought all her goods in pennyworths and became generally known as "Peg Pennyworth." She left a fortune of over £100,000. There are lesser characters, too, who are worthy of note, like the centenarian, Ann Keighley of Hunslet, who when she died left 253 grandchildren and great-grandchildren, and a certain woman still commemorated by a brass in Catterick church, who had the rather grim habit of carrying a winding sheet with her wherever she went. Our county has not lacked women of originality.

Village Rhymes

IN days when every village kept itself to itself there was local rivalry between neighbouring communities. As in the rhyme which said:

Runswick men wi' all their toil
Cums ti' Staithes to sell their oil.

To which the answer was:

Steeathes men wi' all their nuts
Gans ti' Runswick to fill their guts.

At Market Weighton long ago there was a dissolute parson who presumably had a bad influence on the parish, for a verse was circulated in the district naming the cleric:

Market Weighton,
Robert Leighton,
Brick church and wooden steeple
Drunken priest on wicked people.

Local feeling was expressed too, in the North Riding:

If you wish to find a fool
And do it wi'out mistake;
Tak' t'first you meet in Stillington
In Easingwold or Crayke.

Bedale could stand up for itself for in the words of its own past:

Bedale bonnets and Bedale faces
Find nowt ti' beat 'em
In onny places;
For t'first are fairings
And t'last are Graces.

"Fairings," of course, were presents bought for young ladies at annual hirings and fairs.

Of Skipton you were warned:

Skipton in Craven
Is never a haven
But many a day of foul weather,
And he that would say to a pretty girl, may,
I wish for his cravat a tether.

When Halifax began to build houses of the new-fangled bricks in the 18th century there was a verse penned in nearby Heptonstall which went:

Halifax is built o' wax
Heptonstall o' stone.

To which a Halifax man added the scathing lines:

I' Halifax ther's bonny lasses,
I' Heptonstall ther's nooan.

Buried Treasure

TREASURE hunting usually stirs thoughts of sunken galleons, pirate gold and curiously drawn maps bearing the words "X marks the spot." But there are more mundane

ways of discovery. A servant girl living near Aysgarth in the 1920s had a dream that money was buried in a nearby field. She found the place next day and began digging. Her faith in dreams was justified when she unearthed a bronze urn containing coins which she distributed to her friends.

It is certainly true that during the time of the Dissolution of the monasteries, a good deal of the wealth of our abbeys and religious houses was hidden in the hope that it would be recovered when the monasteries were rebuilt. Few of them ever were, so it is possible that some still remains to be found. A century or so ago, when a vicarage in North Yorkshire was being rebuilt, a workman reported to have found a large box of coins of the time of Henry VI and later. The value ran into many thousands of pounds. When he refused to part with his find he was imprisoned in York Castle. It was believed at the time that the hoard was part of the possessions of Guisborough Priory.

At Whitby there is a local tradition that when St. Hilda's Abbey was despoiled, many of its valuables were put on a ship in the harbour to be carried to London. The vessel and its cargo were wrecked at the harbour bar, so there may still be treasure to be found. There are many legends of such lost or buried gold in Yorkshire but for the most part they have remained legends. It used to be said that anyone who ran three times round Middleham Castle, in Wensleydale, would find buried treasure if he dug at the place where he had stopped. It all depended of course on where he started. More widely known is the story that a hoard of treasure is buried under a staircase in the now derelict Dob Park Castle, in the Washburn valley off Wharfedale. The only obstacle here is a three-headed dog which is said to guard it. Kirkstall Abbey, Pen Hill in Wensleydale, and Bolton Priory all have somewhat similar stories told about them.

The strangest treasure-hunting story comes, however, from Upsall Castle in the Vale of Mowbray, of which only a frag-

Middleham Castle

ment of the original building remains. A man from Upsall village who had an obsession about buried gold dreamed three nights in succession that if he stood on London Bridge he would hear something to his advantage. So he set out on foot to fulfil his dream. Footsore and weary, many days later he sat on the bridge still optimistic. There he was accosted by another man who asked him why he waited. He told of his dream and his listener was highly amused for he, in turn, said he had had a curious dream which told him to dig under a certain bush in the castle grounds of a place called Upsall in Yorkshire. But as he had never heard of the place he was not inclined to search. Back home tramped the man from Upsall, dug beneath the bush, and there was a crock of gold with an inscription on it which, when translated, read:

Look lower—where this stood
Is another twice as good.

So he dug and there was another, and after that another.

Twelfth Night Revels

TWELFTH Night seems to be little observed in Yorkshire in these times, except that most people make sure that the holly and the mistletoe are taken down on that night—to omit

to do this is said to bring bad luck. Yet it was once almost as important as Christmas itself. At Brough they used to set up a small tree in the middle of the town with torches fixed to its branches. These were lit while the local band played, and then there used to follow a "rough and tumble" to gain possession of the tree and carry it to one of the three inns of the town. The inn that won became the scene of the rest of the evening's revels.

Up to about a century ago the Night was celebrated in Leeds by visits of friends and relations to one another's houses for the playing of cards and the drinking of the "wassail cup." An old custom for the evening was to eat a cake in which a bean was hidden, the finder being "king of the revels" for the evening.

At Burley-in-Wharfedale they held a Feast of the Great Pudding on Twelfth Night, attended by villagers from the district around. About 30 stones of flour and a similar weight of fruit were used in making a huge plum pudding which, when boiled, was distributed from a platform erected under the great elm tree near the *Malt Shovel Inn.* It was said that though the pudding was boiled for several nights and days it was never possible to cook it thoroughly, and that those who stood below to receive it were usually well plastered with it as it was handed down to them by the carvers, and some fierce scrambles took place. We seem to take our pleasures much more sadly in these days.

The Missing Bride

OLDER readers may recall the time when *The Mistletoe Bough* was one of the most popular drawing-room ballads because of its pathetic story. It had many variations in its telling but the general theme was that of a beautiful girl at a party after her wedding. There was much gaiety and feasting and many congratulations for the bride and bridegroom. Just before the party broke up it was suggested that they should all play the old game of hide-and-seek with the bride hiding from the rest. She remembered an old oak chest in the hall and hid herself inside. But alas she could not open the lid again and her voice was not strong enough to be heard in the merriment.

The guests searched high and low for the girl but she could

not be found. Her disappearance broke the heart of the bridegroom and he died shortly afterwards. Many years elapsed before the old oak chest was opened and the skeleton was found in the remains of the wedding dress.How and when this story originated (long before it became a popular ballad) is unknown. It has been variously attributed to Minster Lovell in Oxfordshire and to the Lovell family of Skelton in North Yorkshire.

"Wonderful Predictions"

ONE of the most popular broadsheets sold in the streets some 300 years ago bore the title *Wonderful Predictions, declared in a Message as from the Lord, to his Excellency, Sir Thos. Fairfax and the Councell of his Army.* It was published in London in 1648 and was illustrated by two woodcuts, one a portrait of Fairfax and the other representing a portrait of the Rev. John Saltmarshe, prophesier, depicted in a winding sheet and holding a lighted torch. Frederick Ross in his *Celebrities of the Yorkshire Wolds*—published nearly a hundred years ago—tells the story of this fanatical Puritan, believed to be of the Saltmarshe family of Howden:

"It is said that on the morning of December 4th, 1647, he told his wife that he had been in a trance and had received a message from God which he must deliver immediately to the army, and mounting his horse he rode to London and thence to Windsor where being introduced to the Council of Officers, he told them that the Lord had left them and would destroy them by internal dissention for having sought to destroy his people, who had stood by them in their greatest difficulties. He then went to the General and told him that God was highly displeased with him for having committed his saints to prison. A similar message he delivered to Cromwell and departed, taking leave of the officers, saying that they would not see him again."

On his return journey he called on several friends, bidding them farewell, telling them that his work on earth was at an end, and asking them to take care of and be kind to his wife. When he saw his wife he was apparently in perfect health, but said there was nothing more for him to do but die, which he did on December 11th, 1647.